The Sylph

*Or Madame de R***'s Dream, written
by herself to Madame de S****

Claude Prosper Jolyot de Crébillon (fils)

Translated by Richard Robinson

Sunny Lou Publishing Company
Portland, Oregon, USA
http://www.sunnyloupublishing.com

2nd Edition: April 7, 2024
Original Publication Date: October 16, 2021

ISBN: 978-1-955392-66-2

* * *

This translation from French is based on Chez Prault Fils' edition of *Le Sylphe, ou Songe de Madame de R*** écrit par elle-même à Madame de S****, Paris, 1735.

Contents

A Foreword

It was about one week ago, give or take a day or two; I had no intention of translating a book, let alone a short story, by Claude Prosper Jolyot de Crébillon (*fils*); in fact, I had entirely forgotten about this dear artist, not being in my right libertine mind at the time. I was between translations, and working on something else, something fine, something personal, when a person I do not know, but do now, contacted me out of the blue – like some elemental spirit fallen purposefully out of a Paracelsian blue sky, – asking us whether we had any intention of translating something from the Crébillon canon, with a suggestion of *Le Sylphe*.

The request was not as random as one might at first suppose, not random at all really, given the publishing house has several 18th-century French libertine works on the books, and more to come, books on the books, if you will – you can count them on the decrepit fingers of one old Frenchman's hand I believe.

Looking into the request, it was found to have merit, arch merit, and this little gem of a work which had so far, – so far as we know – for 300 years now nearly, eluded English translators, eludes them NO MORE. And *fiat!*

– Richard Robinson (October 2021)

The Sylph

Or Madame de R***'s Dream, written by herself to Madame de S***

You are wrong to complain of my silence, Madame, & it is not enough of an excuse to accuse someone of laziness when one has just come out of one's own. How annoying I would be to you if my exactitude forced you sometimes to write me! you would scarcely have time to think: consider, – perhaps you have never thought about it, – that there is no more active idleness than yours in the world. The commotion of Paris, which does not leave you a moment's leisure to form a clear idea, the non-stop pleasures, the countless company that one mixes with & which always amuses, however ridiculous that might be; the habits of our well-bred people, the impertinence & insipidness of our dandies, who for the most part are always found together, a bizarre contrast, at Court as well as in the City. The adventures that occur, & which perpetually furnish the occasions for scandalmongering, the occupations of the heart that divert, even when they hold no interest. The time so agreeably spent on one's toilette by our young Senators. The ever varied pleasure that coquetry brings, the game that fills one's time & mind when the desertion of a Lover or the considerations of charity leave time on one's hands: Eh, how! how is it that in all that hustle & bustle you could sometimes think of me? You reproach me for my taste for solitude; if you only knew how agreeably I spend my time, you would visit me to take part in my amusements, however unreal they might be. You will laugh at me, clearly, when I acknowledge that these pleasures that I praise so highly are nothing but dreams; yes, Madame, they are dreams; but there are some dreams whose illusion brings us real happiness, & whose flattering memory contributes more to our felicity than those habitual pleasures that constantly recur, & that weigh on our minds in the midst even of the desire we have to enjoy them fully.

You know that I have, for the longest time now, passionately desired to see one of those elementary spirits, known to us by the name of Sylphs: I have always thought that there was nothing in the din of Cities that might sufficiently attract them to put in an appearance, & can you blame them? Thus the idea that led me so often to the countryside & made me so haughtily reject the whisperers of sweet nothings: perhaps, if not for the desire I had to be worthy of the love of a Sylph, I would have succumbed to them? For some of those whisperers are quite fetching; I do not regret my severity however, for it has brought me to my goal, which is a dream; I will not tell you my adventure except in that light, & you must deal with your incredulity. However, if it were a dream, I would have remembered having fallen asleep before it occurred; I would have been aware of waking, & then what other explanation than a dream would have caused what I am about to relate to you? How would I have retained the Sylph's discourse so well? It is not natural that I should have imagined what you are about to hear, all these ideas that were never familiar to me: Oh, assuredly, I did not dream! You are free to believe whatever you wish; as for me, I will not use expressions like "it seemed to me" or "I believe I saw"; I will say, "I was," "I saw..."; but enough of this preamble.

Toward the end of last week, I had retired to my room; the night was warm. I went to bed in a modest fashion, for someone who believes she is alone, but would not have done so if I had thought someone was watching me. Tired of the Provincial company of people I had to put up with for most of the day, I sought some compensation in a book of moral instruction, when I distinctly heard pronounced, albeit in a half voice, & with a sigh: "Oh God, what charms!" Those words surprised me; & putting down my book, I attempted, despite the fright that began to seize me, to prick up an ear; not hearing another thing in my room, I thought I had been mistaken & imagined to myself that my distracted mind was giving presence to what I had just read: however, it was not likely to have been found in the moral instruction; moreover, at that moment I could think of nothing that might fit. I was still plunged in these thoughts when I heard, more distinctly than before: "O mortals! Are you made for her possession!?" However flattering those words might be, they redoubled my fear, & returning in a hurry to my bed, I pulled the sheet over my head, half dead with fright, & in such a state as a fearful woman might find herself in. "Ah, cruel woman!" it exclaimed then, "why conceal yourself from my sight? what do you fear from someone who adores you, & who unfortunately for himself is so respectful that he does not dare employ violence to see you; answer me at least, do not make your lover despair." Alas! I responded in a hushed voice; what could I say, finding myself in such surprising circumstances! "But what can you possibly have to fear from me?" it replied, "I have already told you that I adore you; rest assured, I will not show myself; & although your sight of me could banish the fear you have in your soul, I do not wish to expose you just yet to the surprise that it will cause you." Reassured a little by these words, I slowly let down the bedsheet; I realized that this was only a matter of a declaration of love, & I recalled with pride that it wasn't the first time I had received one. I do not have a weak soul, & besides I did not think I had anything to fear from an adventure that began in this way. However, someone was in love, I was alone & in a situation where I had everything to fear from an enterprising person, & to whom I attributed more strength than a man possesses. That reflection disquieted me, I immediately saw the risk I was running, & I saw it with all the more fear, given I had no means to protect myself. It was one of those awkward situations in which virtue served for absolutely nothing; I imagined also that it was a spirit that was speaking to me, & at first I imagined it impalpable; but that spirit had feelings, it loved me: what would prevent it from assuming a body? all those ideas held me in a state of never-ending irresolution, when the voice began again: "I know everything that's going on in your soul, my beautiful Countess; I will be respectful, we never act except when we are loved." Good, I said to myself, I do not believe I will ever put you in a position of needing to show disrespect. "Do not respond," said the voice; "we are somewhat dangerous Lovers, for we know everything that goes on in the heart of a woman; it cannot come up with any desires that we might not satisfy; we enter into all its caprices, we sunset its Rivals, & we augment its charms; we know all its foibles, & when it lets out a sigh of love, which nature in a moment of distraction finds at its strongest, we seize on it; in a word, the faintest idea of temptation becomes, by our efforts, a violent temptation, & soon satisfied; admit that if men possessed our science, not a single woman could escape them. Add to that that our invisibility works against jealous husbands, or ridiculous mothers, with marvelous resource; & there are no means to prevent it; no prying eyes that can discover this secret; but for God's sake," he added, "stop trying to hide yourself from me, that scrupulousness will do you no good, given that you will see me only when you want to, & that your feelings for me depend solely on you." With those words, I showed myself; & the spirit, for he was a spirit, let out such a cry on seeing me that it made me think to go back under the sheet; I steeled my nerve however. "Ah!" he cried, on seeing me, "what beauties! too bad they were destined for a base mortal! It is impossible that they might escape me." What! I said to him, do you think that I won't escape you? "Yes, of course, I think that." I find, I retorted, quite a bit of presumption in that idea. "You are mistaken; you have much less familiarity with your heart than I do: all women think the same way, they have the same feelings, the same desires, the same vanity, & more or less the same reflections; & those reflections are always weak when it is question of a penchant." But, virtue, I said to him, do you believe virtue is pointless? "It would not seem to be," he responded, "& yet, I imagine that you practice it very little." You have too poor an idea of us, I said, to think us incapable of the least reflection. "No," he responded, "I believe that you reflect, but your heart is more active & quick on the uptake, it escapes reflection, & feelings take the upper hand over reason with you. It's not that you don't think enough to know what you need to avoid; conflicts arise in your heart, you sustain them for a while, & you succumb to them finally with this consolation that if your heart had been found weaker than you, you would have carried the day." Do you believe, I replied, that we can never conquer our penchant? Are we so cruelly slaves of our passions that nothing can repress them? "That topic," he responded, "would require too long a discussion; I think that it isn't impossible to find virtuous women, but from what I can tell by your commerce as a whole, virtue is not what amuses women the most: you know that one must possess it, & it seems to me that you merely give in to that necessity with regret. One thing that appears to authorize my feeling is the sadness, & the bad mood, that reigns over the face of a virtuous woman, of a prude, of those people who have made themselves virtuous out of pride, to have the pleasure of insulting the weaknesses of their sex. There are times when they pay quite dearly for that pleasure, & they would prefer to be able to renounce it. But what to do? It's a published virtue that one must keep up, they groan in silence; always tempted, they would soon make a pleasure from the temptation that torments them, if they could be sure that their weaknesses were ignored. Their perpetual cries against pleasure demonstrate less the hatred they carry than the regret they have to be deprived of it, by a misunderstood vanity: add to this, that it is rare to find a pretty woman who is a prude, or a prude who is pretty, which condemns her rightly to hold on to that virtue that nobody dares attack, & which incessantly aggrieves the repose in which men let her languish." But, do you think, I said to him, that all women are prudes? "Men," he responded, "would be quite unhappy if there were only women of that character." However, I said, they want us to be virtuous. "That," he said, "is a refinement of taste for those with a sense of duty for their seductions, to destroy a thing that cost them so dearly to establish in your soul, & which suits you so well, whatever you might say. No, that unshakeable virtue is only the grimace of it, but that's what I imagine, & I cannot describe it to you because I have not yet dropped in on someone of that sort." What is it then, I asked him, that men call virtue? "The resistance that you oppose to their desires, & which is born of your attention to a sense of duty." And what is that, I continued? "It is immense," he replied; "but as you abridge it each day, I think nothing remains of it to be seen; today it consists merely in propriety anymore, even if not followed to the letter." Will that disorder last for long? I asked him? "So long," he said, "as women believe virtue to be an ideal, & pleasure real, & I do not see any evidence of them changing their way of thinking. Besides, every woman has some foible, & that foible however well disguised never escapes the unrelenting investigation of her lover. A voluptuous woman abandons herself to the pleasure of the senses. A delicate woman to the charm of feeling her heart occupied. A curious woman to the desire of being instructed. It would cost an indolent woman too much to refuse. A vain woman would lose too much thereby if her charms were ignored; she wants to read the impression she can have on men in a Lover's fierce passion. An avaricious woman cedes to a vile love of gifts. An ambitious woman to stunning conquests, & a coquette to the habit of surrendering." You are quite knowledgeable, I told him; "It is because," he said, "I started early. But weren't you about to go to sleep? This great desire of a philosopher does not sit well in this first encounter, & I am sure that you take me for one of the most novice Sylphs around presently. Who knows whether profiting so poorly from such sweet moments as these that I spend with you does not merit their being given to someone else. A Sylph in love! speaking morality; goodness gracious, pardon me for having employed my time so poorly." I do not know, I responded, how else you would wish to employ it; you have piqued my interest, & I would be quite happy to prove to you that virtue exists. "In other words," he said, laughing, "you possess it but only inconsistently. I have no doubt that you possess it however, & if I hadn't told you earlier all that I think, it is because so beautiful a person as you are offers so many things to praise, that one finds in her presence no time to express it." I do not forgive you for having forgotten to however, I told him; I will make you repent it. "My beautiful

Countess," he replied, "one tells a beautiful woman that she has charms because, by repeating it to her often, it is a polite way of exhorting her to make use of them; but will it do to remind her of her virtue, when it is in our best interest that she forgets it? Besides, no threats: men are fine with all those niceties, but keep in mind that you cannot fool me. It is embarrassing, & I am not at all surprised to see you thinking: a Lover who knows everything you're thinking, who penetrates everything, against whom you are helpless, is something quite awkward." In that case, I said to him, I cannot put up with it, I will not love you. "You will do nothing of the sort," he said, "to avoid loving me; you need only tell me quite seriously to stop seeing you. What is more, you must want it, & that is what you do not want. Curious as you are, you will never be able to stop yourself from seeing this adventure through to the end. You are a hundred percent with me, just like all other women at the beginning of a passion. They know that in order not to succumb, they must run away; but passion pleases, it warms the heart and shuts down reflection; seduction is constant, a return to oneself, momentaneous; pleasure redoubles, virtue disappears, the Lover remains, why run away? & clearly, you will not run away." You appear a little too sure of your conquest, I said; I would like a Lover who is more respectful, & whose desires were a little less bold and treated me better. "In other words," he interrupted, "you would like me to waste my precious time; I'm not made like that." You don't know women that well, clearly! "Assuredly not," he replied. And have you succeeded everywhere that you have confessed your love? "Everywhere? no; I have often been obliged to change appearance to make myself loved; the first woman that pleased me was an innocent young woman who was still afraid of spirits; I took care to speak with her only at night: I thought she would die. Try as I might to convince her that I was an Aerial spirit, that we were beautiful, shapely... the list of our good qualities that I rattled off for her only made her more afraid, & if I hadn't assumed the face of her Music Master, I was lost. The person I addressed next was a Lady of great standing, very ignorant, who understood nothing about celestial substances either, & who was incapable of imagining that I could be a solid body; that idea did me considerable wrong with her. Unable to get over it in spite of herself, I thought that by taking on the resemblance of a very handsome man who loved her I could lead her along; I was wasting my time. Finally, not knowing what else to do, I put myself at her service, & I did myself up so well as a domestic that she would have never taken me for an elementary spirit; & do you know what was bizarre, – it worked! In Spain, I found a woman who, after seeing me, did not want me, & preferred her lover to me; I have yet to be disappointed like that in France. The list of my adventures would be too long; however, I must not forget a learned woman, whose studies focused primarily on Astronomy & Physics. I saw her, & I told her who I was; she was not frightened, but after incredible efforts, I could not persuade her. 'How is it possible,' she said to me, 'if you are corporeal matter in your region, that our atmosphere does not suffocate you when you visit among us; & if your being is composed only of fine vapors that cannot resist impressions of the air, & that the least wind can dissipate, what good are you here?' Far from refuting her argument by discourses, I beseeched her to allow me to prove it to her; she consented, determined, no doubt, by the minuscule risk she believed she ran, or, supposing there was some risk, by the pleasure of having found in rarefied Physical nature something extraordinary that nobody else knew about. I tried to convince her then; but in the time I had hoped she would cede to the force of my arguments – 'Oh God! what an idea!' she shouted. Have you ever seen more stubborn incredulity? At first I was not put off, but given the hour, & the manner in which I spoke to her, she was obstinate; as you will be doubtless, by treating me as a chimera & a dream; I got tired of giving her material to think about, & I left, even though she made me hope for a near conversion; but you," he added, "will you be as incredulous?" I would not be so curious at least, I told him; I am persuaded that I am dreaming; but content in the pleasure that this dream is giving me, I have no desire to know whether it could be true. "And me," resumed the spirit, "I get the feeling that everything is too much truth with you. I no longer wish to expose myself to the danger of seeing your charms, I leave rather unhappy for being unable to make myself loved by you; I will shy away from the rigors that your cruelty prepares for me." How impatient you are! How is it you expect me to love you? Do I even know what you are? "Have you had the curiosity to ask me?" he said. Alas! I responded, I'm afraid to upset you by asking; that, & also the fear that you aren't worse than a spirit, have held me back; but if you allow me, – what are you? "What," he said, "what do you think I am?" I believe, I said, that you are a Spirit, a Demon, or a Magician. But whatever it is that I imagine you to be, I believe you to be something quite friendly & quite unusual. "Would you care to see me?" the spirit asked. No, I said, it is not time: please respond to my questions. What are you? "I am a Sylph." A Sylph! I shouted, transported. A Sylph! "Yes, charming Countess, would you love them?" If I love them!? Great God! But you have got to be kidding me, there is no such thing; or if there is, what can mortals do for your happiness; & so celestial an essence as yours, how can it lower itself to a commerce with humans!? "Our happiness," he said, "bores us when we cannot share it with someone, & all our effort is spent looking for some dear object worthy to attach ourselves to." But, I interrupted him, I have read that Sylphids were so beautiful, why... "I understand you," he said, "why don't we constantly attach ourselves to them? We do not *touch* them enough, they see us too often, & it is always one reason or another; but so as not to let the race of Sylphids die out, they accord us some favors; the same consideration moves us, & as you can see, such things cannot make for the most tender bonds between us. It's akin to how you humans act when you're married. We seek out women who draw us out of our lethargy, just as they seek out men who compensate them for the boredom we cause them. All these things are well defined amongst us, & we let each other follow his penchant without jealousy & without ill humor. You think, – " he added, "admit that it's a pretty fine thing to have a Sylph for a lover. As I mentioned to you earlier, there is not one fantasy that we do not satisfy, not one good that we do not shower them with, those whom we love more like slaves than lovers; we are submissive to their every whim, unbending on one point only." What is that? I asked him brusquely. "We demand constancy, & I can assure you that, with us, the least appearance of infidelity is always followed by the cruelest death." Mercy! I cried, I never want anything to do with you. At this, the spirit broke out into such a laugh that it made me realize the simplicity of my fear. You laugh, my Sylph, I said. "I laugh," he said, "because not a single woman has not acted in the same way on that article, & because they prefer their natural inconstancy to every advantage that our possession assures them." You are mistaken, I said to him; not at all wishing to be inconstant, I have nothing to fear, & yet the idea that I cannot be so without risk, seriously afflicts me. You will always believe that you owe my attachment to you to my fear of punishment only; you will love me less. "Can you believe it!" he responded, "if we make dissembling women uncomfortable because we know everything that they think, those who have a good & correct heart ought to be charmed that nothing escapes us; we take into account those niceties of the soul, those refined feelings that the stupidity & indolence of men do not perceive, & the more we understand their love, the more perfect their happiness becomes. But do not believe that the condition I propose is so terrible. Sylphs are in all respects so well above men that you would be hard pressed to find constantly loving them a torture. I imagine that the boredom of a habit wherein the heart languishes is the only thing that pushes a woman towards inconstancy: she no longer sees in her lover those tumultuous desires the which, whether she repels them or whether she wishes to satisfy them, equally amuse her. He is merely a bored man excited by her propriety, who nonchalantly says that he loves her, who proves it to her with more discomfort still, & whose silent & cold face never succeed in persuading her what his mouth says. What will a woman do in such a case? By a pointless & misunderstood honor, will she pass the rest of her youth in a relationship that no longer makes her happy? She changes, & rightly. She's accused of a crime if she's the first to change; it's because she feels more deeply than men, & because she has no time to lose. Besides, it is often out of kindness for him whom she loved; she sees him languishing next to her without his being able to resolve to leave her, because he fears dishonoring himself; she furnishes the pretext & assumes responsibility for the crime. It's a very generous act & something men don't deserve, for they have the impertinence to get upset over it." Sylphs, I asked him, are not subject to boredom & disgust then? Clearly they are as constant with us as they demand us to be with them. "At least," he responded, "when they change, it happens so quickly that one does not have time to guard against it; they are seen amorous one minute, and a quarter of an hour later they disappear." But someone who guarded against it, & who changed before they did, I said to him, you forget that... ah, I remember now! You are cruel beings to want to deprive us of all our resources. "When you do not have the idea of death constantly before your eyes," he replied, "you do not want to change. The best means to prevent a woman from being inconstant is to give her no time to rely on a caprice; but that care & attention would be too tiresome for humans, & it only belongs to Sylphs to know how to occupy every instant, & to anticipate momentary fantasies that arise in your heart." I believe, I told him, that even with the happy talents you attribute to Sylphs, one can still be disgusted by them; it is good to let us desire sometimes; the time we spend reflecting on our pleasures entertains us more than all the attentiveness of a lover; besides, you admit that perpetual care & attention is tiresome, & that would be enough to prevent me from desiring you, the certitude of never having desired you in vain. "That is a rather unusual sentiment," he said, "& I doubt it's true. Believe me that with us one has no time to make such reflections; you become Sylphids by virtue of your commerce with us, & participating in our substance; the effort you make to respond to our insistences becomes as light for you as it is for them." You know how to remove all difficulties, I said to him; but when you leave a woman, is some essence of you left behind? "Sometimes out of kindness," he responded, "we take some portion of it away with us; but out of malice we often leave the whole kit & kaboodle." That's not good, I replied. "I agree," he said, "we could dispense with leaving behind desires that only we can satisfy, but we have no reason to believe that it is regretted, & that gives us some pleasure. You're thinking." It is true, I said, I'm thinking that I know some female Sylphids in the world. "Oh! really," he said to me, "given it's at Court that we make our greatest strides, it is not difficult to recognize our traces, but it seems to me that that type of malice does not frighten you as much as the death you reacted to earlier; it has its inconveniences though." I'm afraid of them, but I can avoid them. "By not loving me," said the Sylph, "you would gain nothing, it is also the punishment of those who resist us." Eh! Great God, I cried out, where to run, where to hide! "How about we do without all the banter," the Sylph said. Oh! certainly we will do without it, I cried out in a panic: no commerce, Mr. Demon, sir; if you wish to engage me to give you immortality, you would need to hide the perversity of your character & the risks that follow the engagements one has with you. "Let's unpack that a bit," he responded; "I see a mind imbued with the thoughts that the Count de Gabalis has uttered: you believe that you can give us immortality; in other words, that you do what nature did not judge it appropriate for you to do; I also think that according to those beautiful ideas, you believe that we are subject to the feeble lights of your sages, & that we come down at their evocations: what pretense! That an essence superior to that of man should have need of some instruction by him, & could be forced to obey him! As for the immortality that you pretend to be able to give us, that fantasy is even more ridiculous, for frequent commerce with an inferior substance would presumably debase our own, far from giving it new strength." I see, I said to him, that I was too credulous, but that does not make me any more disposed to love you, I'm afraid. "Rest assured," he replied, "as for the death I threatened you with, we don't always go to that extreme, we often change ourselves, & you can return to your prerogatives then; but we do not want to hear about it, any more than you do when you're engaged; those are affronts that you do not pardon, & our vanity is as sensitive as yours. As to the other punishment, unless you yourself ask for it, I will spare you: Look, think it over, dismiss me quite seriously, or accept the conditions I propose to you." How do you expect, I said, that I can be assured of my feelings with someone I do not even know, whom I have never seen? I do not deny that you already please me a little; but if it turned out that you were a Gnome,[1] unfortunately... "Do not speak ill of the Gnomes," interrupted the Sylph. "It is true that they do not possess a comely face, but many a conquest was saved because of them; they are for us what Financiers are for men, & that is not something your sex considers as the least of things. Every day even, they get the better of our Sylphids." How's that! I asked him, a race as superior as yours, influenced by gifts? "Yes," he said, "they take from the Gnomes to give to their Lovers, & when that attention does not oblige them to respond to the passions of those hideous spirits, – they are women after all, & by consequence capricious; change amuses them, & the bizarreness of their taste is a source of pleasure for them, all the more touching as they can be reproached for it. But, my beautiful Countess, isn't there anything more interesting you wanted to speak with me about; & will you always be wrapped up with objects as small as those I have satisfied your curiosity on? Will you not allow me to show myself?" Ah, my Sylph! I exclaimed. I'm so afraid in your presence..., "that you might not desire it!" he said sighing. I myself responded with only a

---

[1]Original footnote: Gnomes: Spirits inhabiting the earth, guardians of its treasures.

sigh. At that moment an extraordinary light filled the room; I saw at my bedside the most handsome young man you can imagine, with majestic traits, & the most gallant & most noble fit. I was surprised to see him, but I was not frightened. "Eh, well," he said, getting down on his knees before me with an attitude full of love & respect, "eh, well, charming Countess, could you swear fidelity to me?" Yes, my dear, my gorgeous Sylph! I cried out, I swear to you an eternal ardor; I fear only your inconstancy. But how could I be worthy of it?... "Your contempt for men, & the secret passion you have for us," he told me, "have influenced mine, it is more tender than you think; I could provoke a dream, & make myself happy in spite of you; but I am thinking about it with more delicacy, & I have decided to owe it all to your heart." Alas! I demonstrated perhaps, at that moment, a little too much weakness for my Sylph, but I adored him. How charming you are, I said to him, & how unhappy I would be if you were an illusion! Is it really true that... Ah! ah!... I can touch you!...

And there I was, Madame, with my Sylph, & I have no idea where my distractions & my transports would have led me if my chambermaid hadn't entered the room right then and there & frightened him off; he flew away: I called after him in vain; his indifference for me makes me think that it was nought but a pleasant illusion that presented itself to my mind, but isn't it a shame if this were merely a dream?

Other Books by the Publisher

Fanchette's Pretty Little Foot by Restif de La Bretonne

Je M'Accuse... by Léon Bloy

My Hospitals & My Prisons by Paul Verlaine

Salvation Through the Jews by Léon Bloy

Words of a Demolitions Contractor by Léon Bloy

Cellulely by Paul Verlaine

Ecclesiastical Laurels by Jacques Rochette de la Morlière

Flowers of Bitumen by Émile Goudeau

Songs for Her & Odes in Her Honor by Paul Verlaine

On Huysmans' Tomb by Léon Bloy

Ten Years a Bohemian by Émile Goudeau

The Soul of Napoleon by Léon Bloy

Blood of the Poor by Léon Bloy

Theresa the Philosopher & The Carmelite Extern Nun by Marquis d'Argens & Anne-Gabriel Meusnier de Querlon

A Platonic Love by Paul Alexis

Two Novellas: Francine Cloarec's Funeral and Benjamin Rozes by Léon Hennique

The Revealer of the Globe: Christopher Columbus & His Future Beatification (Part One) by Léon Bloy

Joan of Arc and Germany by Léon Bloy

Héloïse Pajadou's Calvary by Lucien Descaves

An Immodest Proposal by Dr. Helmut Schleppend

The Pornographer by Restif de La Bretonne

Style (Theory and History) by Ernest Hello

On the Threshold of the Apocalypse: 1913-1915 by Léon Bloy

She Who Weeps (Our Lady of La Salette) by Léon Bloy

www.ingramcontent.com/pod-product-compliance
Lightning Source LLC
Chambersburg PA
CBHW021449240726
R18617000001B/R186170PG48289CBX00001B/1